Under the Serpent Sea

A Magical World Awaits You
Read

THE
SECRETS
OF
DROON

Under the Serpent Sea

by Tony Abbott

Illustrated by Tim Jessell

A
LITTLE APPLE
PAPERBACK

SCHOLASTIC INC.
New York Toronto London Auckland Sydney
Mexico City New Delhi Hong Kong Buenos Aires

For more information about the continuing saga of Droon,
please visit Tony Abbott's website at
www.tonyabbottbooks.com.

Book design by Dawn Adelman

ISBN-13: 978-0-439-20786-7
ISBN-10: 0-439-20786-X

27 26 25 24 23 22 21 20 19 18 17 16   8 9 10 11 12/0

Printed in the U.S.A.   40
First Scholastic printing, May 2001

And again to Dolores,
who makes the fantasy real

Contents

One

A Mystery Dream

"*Kkkk! Boom-ba-boom!*"

Eric Hinkle was jumping on his bed and making noises.

"*Ka-blamma-bam!*"

His friends Julie and Neal were watching him. Julie's mouth was hanging open. Neal's eyes were as big as moons.

"My dream started with a *huge* storm!" Eric said, waving his arms. "Thunder was pounding the house. Rain was coming down in buckets!"

He paused to catch his breath.

Neal gulped. "Don't stop now, man. Tell us everything you saw."

Eric swallowed once and went on. "It could be a dream about Droon," he said, lowering his voice to a whisper. "But the next part is sort of a mystery. You have to tell me what you think."

Julie and Neal both nodded silently.

Droon.

They would never forget the day they discovered the entrance to the magical land of Droon.

First they found a door hidden by some old crates and cartons in Eric's basement.

Then they pulled the door open and piled into a small closet. The next thing they knew — *whoosh!* — the floor vanished and they were standing on a shimmering staircase.

The staircase led down to a strange and wonderful world. In that world, the good wizard Galen and the young princess Keeah battled a nasty sorcerer named Lord Sparr and a mysterious sea witch called Demither.

Since their first adventure, Princess Keeah had become one of their best friends. Sometimes she would send them a magical message asking them to come. At other times the kids would know through their dreams about Droon that Keeah needed them.

"I hope you did dream of Droon," said Julie. "It's been weeks, and I want to go back."

But Eric's latest dream wasn't like any other he'd ever had. It was more like something that had really happened.

"I was small, maybe four years old," Eric began. "The storm was scaring me, so I went to the basement to hide."

"When I'm really afraid, I sort of freak out," said Neal. "I hide my head and hug my blanket, or maybe a pillow —"

"Neal, *shhh*!" said Julie. "Eric, go on."

Eric tried to remember everything. He closed his eyes. Yes, it was coming back to him. . . .

"It was dark in the basement. . . ." he began.

Rain was splashing against the window over the workbench. The apple trees outside whipped around in the wind.

Suddenly — *boom!* — there was a big banging sound. And the closet door burst open!

Bright red light filled the basement.

"I dived behind an old chair!" Eric said.

"Then, right before my eyes, two people stepped out of the closet and into the room."

"Yikes!" Neal gasped. "Who were they?"

Eric told them what he had seen.

One of the figures was a child about his age, dressed all in blue. The other was a grown-up who wore a long dark cloak.

"What is this place?" the child said. It was a girl's voice. *"Are we still in Droon?"*

"No," said the tall one in a voice like a woman's, but very deep and scary. *"Come, we must do this quickly or he will find us."*

"The big bad man?" asked the girl.

"Yes," said the woman. *"I gave you the red light to help you escape him. And I will give you more. But first, follow me."*

"The girl might be Princess Keeah," said Julie.

"Then the big bad man would have to

be Lord Sparr," said Neal. "He's the biggest, baddest man in Droon. But keep going, keep going!"

Eric told them how, in no time, the two strangers were across the basement floor and up the steps. They moved swiftly, as if their feet didn't even touch the floor.

Quietly, carefully, Eric followed them.

The two figures swept up the steps and into the dark living room. They fluttered past the sofa, the coffee table, and the television.

They started up the stairs to the second floor, then up to the attic.

"There was a weird glow under the woman's cloak," Eric told his friends. "She was hiding something, but I couldn't tell what it was."

"So you followed them to the attic," said Neal, reaching for Eric's pillow. "Then what?"

Eric told how he saw the two figures standing under the sloped roof. Before them was a large window looking out the side of the house.

"*I want to go home,*" the girl said, trembling.

"*Soon,*" the woman answered. "*We must do this together. Are you ready?*"

"*Yes.*" The girl held out her hands.

"*This will be the last time,*" the woman said. "*Then you will have my power.*" She touched the girl's hands.

Zzzz! — a bright red light passed between them, then stopped. The girl held up her hands.

"*I have it now,*" she said.

Red sparks shot from her fingertips.

Eric gasped, and the woman turned sharply, showing her face for the first time. Her features were twisted. Her skin was rough and scaly.

"Hurry! Open the window!" she snapped.

The girl moved her hand and, as if by magic, the window sprang open. Cold wind and rain rushed into the attic.

Without another word, both figures spread their arms, ran to the window, and leaped out.

"They flew!" said Eric, bouncing on his bed again. "Over the trees and high over the street. It was so awesome! I think they dipped behind the library, but the storm got too wild to see. Finally, I woke up." He sat down on the edge of the bed. "So what do you think?"

"Whoa," Neal murmured. "I love the flying part. I wonder what it's like having cool powers like that. Not that we'll ever know. . . ."

Julie's eyes shone. "If the girl was

Keeah, I think we're being called back. I think we should go!"

She and Neal jumped to the bedroom door.

But Eric didn't move.

"What's the matter?" asked Neal.

Eric frowned. "Well, our dreams usually come true in Droon. But I was *little* in my dream. So was Keeah. This dream can't come true."

"But what if it's not really a dream?" said Julie, suddenly excited. "What if it's a memory? I mean, maybe it actually *did* happen. And your dream is what you remember —"

Eric stood up. "Of course! I can't believe I didn't think of it. Remember when Keeah said she had been in my basement once before? But nobody could figure out how?"

"Galen and everybody said it was impossible," said Neal.

"Well, maybe it's not so impossible," said Eric. "If my dream really did happen, it proves that Keeah *was* here before!"

The three friends stared at one another.

They were all thinking the same thing.

They needed to get to Droon right away.

In no time they tramped down the stairs to the basement. They began pulling away the cartons blocking the closet door under the stairs.

"But if the girl was Keeah," said Neal, "then the other person was . . ."

Eric shuddered, remembering the woman's strange face. "That voice, the scaly skin. I know who it was. It was Demither. The witch."

They all shivered to think of her.

The witch had a history of doing bad things. Once she transformed into a giant sea serpent and destroyed Keeah's ship.

Another time, she tried to kidnap Keeah's mother, Queen Relna.

"If it was Demither," said Julie, "it would explain how Keeah seems to have witch powers."

"Exactly," said Eric. "Wizard powers give off a blue light. But Keeah also had red powers like Demither. They're sort of wild and dangerous."

"But why were the two of them in your house?" asked Neal. "That's the biggest puzzle."

"And maybe we'll find out today," said Julie.

The kids piled into the closet. Eric closed the door behind them and Neal switched off the light. The room was dark. Then it wasn't.

Whoosh! The floor vanished and they stood at the top of a rainbow-colored staircase.

Together, the three friends descended the stairs. Down they went through a layer of wispy clouds. Below them, the bright orange sun of Droon shone on a magnificent city.

"It's Jaffa City," said Neal. "Right on Keeah's doorstep. We're pretty good at this, you know?"

Eric grinned at his friends. "Yeah, we are."

But as they hurried down the stairs, a sharp wind rose up and nearly blew them off the side.

"Holy cow!" said Julie, struggling to hold on.

Then hard, icy rain began pelting them.

Before they knew it, large black clouds swept across the sky, completely blotting out the sun.

"What's happening?" asked Eric.

"I don't know, but I see Galen's tower,"

said Julie, pointing to a tall tower standing near the city walls. "Let's try to get over there now!"

"Right," said Neal as the sky boomed with thunder. "Maybe Galen has a blanket I can hide under. This is getting scary!"

Two

Day of Night

The kids ran breathlessly from the stairs all the way to the upper room of Galen's magical tower.

Entering, they screeched to a halt.

"And I thought the weather outside was bad," gasped Eric, looking around the room. "There's a snowstorm in here!"

It did look like a snowstorm.

A snowstorm of paper.

Galen, the white-bearded wizard, was making papers fly all over the cluttered room.

"Now where is that prophecy?" he bellowed, snatching at papers, then sending them off again. "Max! Bring Quill! Keeah! Bring my mirror!"

"Um . . . Galen?" said Julie. "Hello. . . ."

The wizard turned and blinked. "Ah, children! This is a black day for Droon. I must discover where this queer storm is coming from. Max! Where are you? And where is *Quill?*"

Scritch-itch! A sharp scratching sound came from across the room.

Galen whirled on his heels. "There you are!"

Max, the wizard's eight-legged spider troll helper, staggered in under the weight of an enormous book. Standing upright in the book was a long, curved feather pen named Quill.

The kids had seen Quill before. He was a magical pen who wrote down everything that happened in Droon. Sometimes he wrote so fast, he wrote the future. He was writing quickly now.

"Hello, friends!" Max chirped, setting the fat book on Galen's table. "I certainly hope Quill can help us get to the bottom of this storm —"

"Oof! Oh, help! Mirror . . . heavy!" groaned a muffled voice behind the children. They turned to see a big silver mirror edging its way into the room. Someone was under it, trying to carry it.

"It's Keeah!" said Julie.

The kids rushed to the princess, helping her set the mirror down in the center of the room.

Keeah smiled. "Thank you!" she said.

When Eric saw Keeah's light blue tunic, he was more convinced than ever that she was the girl in his dream.

"How did you know to come?" she asked.

Neal was so excited he just blurted it out. "Eric dreamed about you! About when you came to the Upper World! With Demither! The witch!"

Instantly, all the papers fluttered to the floor, Keeah's mouth dropped open, and Max fell over.

Galen frowned. "Eric, tell us everything."

Eric took a deep breath and described each detail of his dream. By the time he'd finished, everyone was staring at him.

"We all think it really happened," said Julie.

Keeah turned to Galen. "I remember

being in Eric's basement, but not the rest of it. And *not* the witch!"

The wizard stroked his snow-white beard slowly. "Clearly, Demither gave you some powers, powers that you cannot control yet. That fire at breakfast this morning, for instance. Or the snakes in my silver washbasin . . ."

Keeah frowned. "I'm sorry about that," she said. "I don't know how any of that happened."

"Exactly the reason we must be careful," said Galen. "Though why the witch gave you powers at all is still the most puzzling of puzzles. I only wish you remembered more of it —"

Kkkkk! A jagged bolt of lightning flashed outside the tower's windows, illuminating the black sky.

"But I see we have more pressing concerns!" Galen said. "Mirror — awake! Show me where this storm comes from."

Zzzzt! There was a loud buzzing sound, and the gray surface of the old mirror cleared.

It showed a rocky coast whipped by rain and wind. Just beyond the jagged cliffs a dark sea was spinning into an enormous swirl of water.

"A hurricane," said Julie. "A big one."

"That must be the center of the storm," said Eric. "But what's out there?"

"More like *who's* out there," said Max, his orange hair standing on end. "That is the Serpent Sea, off the coast of Mintar. Known as the home of Witch Demither!"

Keeah peered into the mirror. "Do you think she's *causing* the storm? But how . . . and why?"

Scritch! Scratch! The magic feather pen suddenly began writing in the book.

"Ah!" said the wizard. "Quill will tell us all!"

The feather pen whizzed furiously across two full pages, then stopped. It seemed to Eric that the pen breathed heavily, and then lay down on the book to take a nap.

Galen read the pages. His face turned pale.

"Master, what's wrong?" asked Max.

The wizard shook his head. "Quill says this storm is indeed the work of Demither —"

"I knew it!" chirped Max. "It's some evil new plan to make the good people of Droon suffer!"

"But there is more," said Galen quietly. "Quill writes that Demither is using the Red Eye of Dawn to cause this storm."

"Oh, man, does it get any worse?" Neal groaned.

The Red Eye of Dawn was a magic jewel created by Lord Sparr to control the forces of nature.

He was planning to use the Eye to help him conquer all of Droon for himself. Then Witch Demither stole the Eye from him.

Now she was using it to make the storm.

Boom-ba-boom! Thunder rumbled overhead, shaking the tower from top to bottom.

"It feels like the end of the world," said Julie, shivering. "What can we do?"

All eyes turned to Galen.

"It is quite clear what you must do," he said. "You must go to Demither's realm under the Serpent Sea of Mintar. There you must stop her from using the Red Eye. Steal it from her if you have to."

Keeah turned to her friends. "Mintar is on the far side of Droon. Will you come with me?"

Eric nodded. "I think that's why we're here!"

"Good," she said with a smile. "Luckily, Friddle the inventor has set up his workshop nearby. He'll help us get to Demither's lair. Follow me!"

She marched quickly out the door.

As Eric, Julie, and Neal went to follow her, Galen raised his hand. "A moment please, my friends. I must tell you of something else that Quill wrote. A warning."

Eric shot a look at Neal and Julie.

"What kind of warning?" he asked.

Galen read from the book. "Quill writes that Keeah will undergo a dangerous trial today. Her powers will be tested as never before. If Keeah fails her trial, it could mean doom for her."

"What kind of trial?" Eric asked.

"What kind of *doom*?" asked Neal.

Galen scratched his brow and went on. "Every young wizard is tested to see if they are worthy of their power. Unfortunately, Keeah possesses not only the good wizard arts but also the angry red arts of the witch. If she becomes afraid or angry, her powers may overwhelm her."

"If that happens," said Julie, "does it mean she might never become a real wizard?"

"Or worse," Galen replied. "The dark powers might turn her against us. And against Droon."

The three friends stared at one another.

"What can we do to help?" asked Eric.

"Alas," said Galen, "Quill warns us not to tell Keeah about this. It might only make matters worse. Also, since I myself would be tempted to help Keeah, I cannot go with you."

"You're not coming?" Julie said. "We're going to the witch's house and you won't be there?"

The wizard gave a half smile. "Perhaps I can find a way around that. Now go stop Demither from using the Eye. And stay close to Keeah."

"We'll stick to her like cheese on a pizza," said Neal. "You can count on us."

"Same here," said Eric. "What Neal said."

The three kids ran down through the tower. When they popped out below, Max was there.

"Children!" he chirped. "Do not let my master join you on your mission today. Quill says he may not."

"I think we'd notice him," said Julie.

"Ah, but Galen is tricky!" said Max. "He is a wizard, after all. He may not look like himself."

"You mean he'd come in disguise?" said Neal. "Like with blue eyebrows? Or big clown feet? Or a bald head? Or the ultimate disguise, glasses?"

Max blinked at Neal. "Just so. But if you see him, bop him right on the nose! He hates that."

"Bop him?" asked Julie. "Bop Galen's nose?"

"What if it's a fake nose?" asked Neal.

"Either way!" Max said. "If he meddles with the prophecy, it may mean *doom* for Keeah!"

Neal grumbled, "There's that word again."

Three

Fasten Your Sea Belts!

Blam! Zzzz! Plink!

Strange noises were coming from a small hut at the edge of the forest just outside the city.

Eric, Julie, and Neal rushed to join Keeah at the tiny door. It creaked as they opened it. *Errrch!*

Inside the hut, they found a short man whose friendly smile, thick glasses, and very large ears they had seen before.

It was Droon's master inventor, Friddle. He bowed to them. "Welcome, all of you!"

As tall as Galen's tower was, the inventor's workshop was long and low. It was filled from wall to wall with odd devices and contraptions.

Neal's eyes lit up, and he began touching everything. "This is the awesomest cool stuff!"

"The ultimate workshop," Eric agreed.

"Friddle, we're on a mission," said Keeah. "We need to get to the coast of Mintar."

"Oh, dear!" said the inventor, running his hands through his fuzzy green hair. "To Witch Demither's underwater realm, eh? You'll need something to get you down to her secret palace."

"And back up again, right?" asked Julie.

"Most definitely," said Friddle.

"What's this thing?" Eric asked, pointing to a thick belt with several compartments on it.

"Ah, I call it my sea belt," the inventor said. "The green button helps you dive. The yellow button brings you to the surface — Neal?"

From the worktable, Neal had picked up a pair of big round glasses. "Wow! These make everything magically blurry. What are they?"

Friddle frowned. "My extra pair of glasses! Now pay attention, please. Each of you must take a sea belt. But whatever you do, don't touch the red button on the belt."

"Why not?" asked Neal, picking up a belt and tapping lightly on the red button.

"Never mind!" said Friddle sharply. "It's not perfected yet, so don't try it. Now follow me!"

Whoosh! Icy wet wind blew into the workshop as Friddle opened the tiny back door.

Outside the hut stood a large bulky shape covered completely by a huge brown cloth.

"What's under there?" asked Keeah.

"Oh, wait till you see!" said Friddle, tugging the cloth until it billowed to the ground.

He beamed. "I present . . . my Flying Flapper!"

What sat before them was a plane. But it was unlike any plane the kids had seen before.

Two thin, rounded wings were attached to each side of a long skinny frame. Five cushioned seats were set inside from front to back. And a big wooden propeller stuck out of the flat nose.

Julie jumped with excitement. "It looks

just like a big bug. It reminds me of a drag-onfly!"

Friddle giggled at Julie. "What a mar-velous name! *Dragonfly* it is. It flies by yip-yip power!"

He tapped a round cage at the front of the plane. In the box were two large balls of blue fur.

Keeah peered closer at the fur balls. "Yip-yips? Why do you call them —"

"Yip! Yip!" cried the creatures loudly. "Yip!"

The princess laughed. "Never mind."

The moment the blue fur balls awoke, they began running in their cage. When they did, the propeller on the plane's front began to turn.

Friddle climbed into the pilot's seat. "Hop aboard the *Dragonfly*, adventurers!"

The four friends piled in, Friddle pulled

levers and pushed buttons, and — *yip-yip-yip!* — the plane shot forward.

It bounced roughly along the ground as the double sets of wings flapped wildly. The instant they lifted off, the storm spun dark air around the plane. Swirling mist covered everything.

"The storm is fierce," said Friddle nervously. "I can't see where we are! What's ahead?"

"I see something," said Neal. "It's . . . it's . . . yikes! A tree! A big one! We're going to hit it!"

Suddenly, a blast of red light shot from Keeah's hands and the tree burst into flames and crashed straight to the ground.

The plane cleared it easily.

"Oh, dear!" Keeah cried. Instantly, she muttered words under her breath. A spiral of blue light swept over the fallen tree and set it upright again, its leaves greener than before.

"I'm so sorry!" she said. "Oh, what would my mother think of me having such powers!"

"The queen would be very proud," said Friddle, pulling the plane up from the city. "For one thing, you are quite brave to make this journey!"

Keeah's mother, Queen Relna, was one of Droon's greatest wizards. But she was under a terrible spell, cursed to change into one animal after another. Most recently she was a dolphin.

Eric gazed at Keeah. He wondered if her mother had been tested as she was going to be. He wished he could tell her what Galen had said about the trial she was going to endure.

But maybe the wizard was right.

Keeah's powers *were* very sensitive.

Besides, if someone did try to help her, they might only make things worse. No, the best thing was to stick close to her, as Neal had said.

Like cheese on a pizza.

For the next two hours the plane soared over Droon. Through the storm they spotted the frosty Ice Hills of Tarabat, the lush Bangledorn Forest, and the rolling deserts of Lumpland.

Suddenly Friddle slapped his hands together in glee. "Ah! Going into Demither's mysterious realm! The danger! The excitement! The danger!"

"Um . . . you said *danger* twice," said Neal.

"There'll be plenty to spare!" said Friddle.

At that moment, they flew over the jagged cliffs of Mintar.

"My gosh," Keeah murmured. "There it is!"

A black tower of wind and water roared up from the green sea, swirling the waves and spinning dark clouds all around it.

"The center of the storm!" said Friddle. "Now remember what I told you about your sea belts. I've brought some helmets for you, too. With them, you'll be able to breathe and talk underwater. When I fly close, you jump out and dive into the water. If I am right, you will find Demither's lair right under the hurricane!"

As they tightened their belts and donned their helmets, Neal laughed nervously. "I never expected to go skydiving in scuba gear. I hope everything works right."

Eric was about to respond when he spotted something on the horizon. "What's that?"

Darkness was spilling up over the edge of the sea, turning the waves from green to black.

"Holy cow," said Julie, squinting. "It's . . . ships. Hundreds and hundreds of ships. Black ones. And they're coming this way."

"Who would be crazy enough to be out in this hurricane?" asked Neal. "Besides us, I mean."

"Whoever it is, you must hurry!" Friddle shouted. "The hurricane is growing stronger. My poor wings are being torn apart. And the yip-yips are getting tired. You must jump now!"

"Then let's go!" said Keeah.

Climbing out onto the tail of the

Dragonfly, the four friends held hands tightly.

The plane dipped into the swirling tower of wind and water.

The kids shut their eyes.

And they jumped.

Four

Into the Creepy Deep

"Ahhhh!"

They all screamed at the top of their lungs.

But their cries were lost in the winds spinning inside the hurricane. They hit the water hard.

Splash-splash-splash-splash!

"Try to stay together!" Eric cried out.

"Good luck!" shouted Neal. "Someone pulled the plug! We're going down!"

And down they went, into the churning waters of the Serpent Sea. Bubbles rushed around them, and strong currents spun them faster and faster.

Pressing the green buttons on their belts steadied them. They drifted down quickly and soon hit the bottom. *Thud-thud-thud-thud*.

Far above them, the ocean's surface swirled angrily from the hurricane. Down below, the water was calmer. It rippled with soft green light.

Gangly plants quivered and waved at them.

"Is everyone okay?" Julie called. Her voice carried through the water to the other helmets.

Eric scrambled up next to Neal, a thin stream of bubbles floating up from his helmet. "All in one piece," he said.

"Then let's get going," said Keeah. "We

have to find Demither's palace. And we don't have much time —"

Rrrr! Just then the ground rumbled, red light flashed through the water, and the storm above spun even faster.

"Demither's playing games," said Julie.

"Well, she'd better not win!" said Neal, gulping loudly inside his helmet as they pressed on in search of Demither's lair.

The first thing they came upon was the wreck of a giant ship. Seaweed sprouted from the deck. Fish swam in and out of the cracks in its hull.

"Many ships have met their doom in Demither's waters," said Keeah. "I'll take a look."

She swam away to the front of the ship.

"Met their *doom*?" said Neal. "I'm really getting to not like that word —"

"Neal, don't freak out," said Eric. "It's scary, sure. But we need to help Keeah. She's the one on trial, remember. So let's stick together."

"Together, huh?" said Neal. "Where's Julie?"

Eric looked around. Julie was nowhere to be found. "Julie —"

"Oh!" came a cry from behind them.

They spun around to see Julie disappearing into the ship, a long tentacle coiled around her.

"Something's got her!" cried Neal.

They swam over as fast as they could. Inside the wreck Julie was cornered by a long snakey creature with fins all over its head. Two eyes burned fiercely on either side of a red snout.

It let Julie go when Eric and Neal barged in.

All of a sudden, bubbles spurted from Julie's air tube. She was laughing inside her helmet.

Then she swatted the monster's red nose.

"Eerrgh!" The creature let out a loud cry, then slithered away into the shadows.

Neal gasped. "Whoa! That was either the bravest thing in the world or the dumbest! That was one ugly sea monster!"

Julie laughed again. "That was no sea monster. It was Galen! Did you see that fake red nose? Max said to bop Galen if we saw him. So I did!"

"Yeah, but are you sure it was —" Eric began.

Kkkk-kkk! Light flashed again, sending strong shock waves through the ship.

An instant later, Keeah was there. "I found something you have to see," she said. "Hurry!"

They followed Keeah over a range of hills jutting up from the ocean floor.

Then they saw it.

A giant dome of rippling green glass.

It spread for miles across the ocean floor.

"It sure is big," said Julie.

Inside the dome were giant sea caves, buildings made of red coral and blue stone, and long, curving bridges of shiny white shells.

"I think we found Demither's lair," said Eric.

"No," said Neal, "it just found us!"

The water sizzled with electricity, and suddenly sea creatures appeared on every side of them.

They looked like sharks except that they had many legs and two sharp tails curling up behind them. Moving swiftly, the creatures coiled a chain of spiky sea-weed around the children.

"We're trapped," said Julie. "Should we fight?"

Keeah's fingers lit up with red sparks. Then she shook her head. "We could. But maybe we want to be captured. If these are Demither's guards, they could lead us to her."

Eric was relieved not to fight the creatures.

"Keeah's right," he said. "The sooner we find Demither, the sooner we get out of here and back on dry land."

"I like that idea," said Neal.

The princess put down her hands.

As she did, a pair of giant rocks nearby split open to reveal a dark watery cave. The creatures' noises made it clear what the children should do.

"I guess we go in the cave," said Keeah.

"I guess we do," said Eric.

The creatures tugged on the chain of seaweed, and the children entered the cave. The walls inside were carved here and there with scenes of a terrible sea serpent attacking ships.

"They call Demither the serpent queen," Julie mumbled. "Now I see why. She rules this place."

Neal nodded. "The first time we saw her, she was a sort of mermaid. The next time she was a serpent. I sure hope she's being her mermaid self today, because her serpent self scares me!"

The twin-tailed creatures led them through the cave and into the green dome itself.

The kids swam up into a pool and stepped out onto a stone plaza. The floor around them was inlaid with rich green and blue tiles and golden stones. Looking up, Eric saw the hurricane still whirling fiercely above them.

"We can take off our helmets here," said Keeah. "There's air."

The kids removed their helmets and hooked them to their belts.

From inside, the dome looked like a big glass bowl turned upside down. In its center stood a palace of emerald-green glass. Five stone towers surrounded the palace, their tops made of spiraling shells.

In every free spot, lush seaweed gardens grew wildly. Pools and fountains bubbled everywhere. And instead of streets, blue-water canals meandered slowly toward the central palace.

The sea creatures ushered the kids across the square and into the green palace. Inside was a throne room unlike any other that they had seen.

The throne itself was a giant scallop shell. Its top was open and curved over a silvery pool.

On each side of the throne were urns blazing with green flames that leaped and fell when the children entered.

The sea beasts removed the chain binding the kids, then slid over to the pool and waited by it.

"Nice place for a not-nice person," Julie whispered. "I wonder what she'll do with us."

Suddenly there was a splash in the pool and something slithered out onto the throne.

It had the head and arms of a woman, but the scaly tail of a fish. She might have looked like a mermaid, except for her rough face and cold expression.

"It's her!" Eric whispered.

It was her. The sea witch. Demither.

"So . . . you have come to my world," the witch said in a raspy voice. "I knew my hurricane would attract your attention."

Eric was sure he'd heard that voice before.

In the dream that was more than a dream.

In Demither's hand was a long staff with an iron claw at its head. In the grip of the claw was a bright crimson stone.

"The Red Eye of Dawn," said Demither, thrusting the staff into a holder by her throne.

At those words, a bolt of sizzling flame burst from the red jewel and crackled over their heads.

"Yes!" said the witch. "The Red Eye of Dawn is alive — and it is angry!"

Five

Black Fire, White Wings

Keeah stepped toward the witch's throne. She narrowed her eyes and spoke.

"Demither, you must stop this storm. We will take the Red Eye of Dawn if we have to —"

"Take the jewel," said the witch softly. "I only wish you could. . . ."

Keeah blinked. "Uh . . . excuse me?"

The witch raised her sunken eyes to the children. She looked different from the last time they'd seen her. She had once seemed very powerful. But now her skin, usually sea green in color, looked almost yellow. Her lips were thin and pale.

"She seems . . . sick," whispered Eric.

"The Red Eye of Dawn has done this to me," Demither said. "It will do it to you, too."

Keeah glanced at her friends, then back at the witch. "What do you mean?"

In the pale light of the green fire, Demither began. "Sparr created this red jewel. I stole it, hoping to gain more power. Ha! Only then did I discover the evil spirit who dwells in the Eye. A spirit more terrifying than I ever imagined."

The children looked at one another.

Keeah said nothing.

"What kind of spirit?" Julie asked finally.

"His name is Om," said the witch.

"Lord Sparr conjured him long ago to destroy whoever possesses the jewel. Even now, Om is draining my power from me. And the Eye grows stronger."

Neal nudged Julie. "It's true," he said softly. "She doesn't look too good."

The jewel pulsed slowly with light.

"See," said the witch. "Even in his sleep, Om listens to his evil master . . . Sparr."

"But Sparr vanished," said Eric. "We heard he almost died. No one has seen him for months."

That was true. The sorcerer had been hurt by another of his terrible creations, the Golden Wasp. After that, he had simply disappeared.

"When the Wasp attacked him, Sparr was changed, perhaps forever," the witch replied, drawing slow breaths. "Not even I know what he looks like now. But he is alive. And he is coming for the Eye."

"Let me guess," said Julie. "He wants the Eye so he can try to take over Droon again."

The witch nodded slowly. "That is why I have used my magic to conjure the Doom Gate."

Neal squeaked. "Is doom, like, *everybody's* favorite word? What's a Doom Gate, anyway?"

"An enchanted prison," said Demither. "Once the Eye is sealed inside it, it can never again be used for evil."

"Evil?" Keeah snapped. "You're a fine one to talk. For all we know, this is a trap that you and Sparr set to capture us!"

Demither narrowed her eyes at the princess. "You do not know me!" she snarled. "It was I who shared my power with you. It was I who stole the Eye from Sparr, stopping his plans to conquer Droon. Yes, and it was *I* who told you your mother was alive!"

"*Then why didn't you stop Sparr from cursing her?*" Keeah said, her fingertips sparking.

"Keeah!" said Eric. "Your powers —"

"Because!" said the witch. "Sparr did not curse your mother — *I did!*"

Keeah gasped sharply and staggered back.

"You . . . you?"

"See for yourself what happened that day at Sparr's fortress," said Demither. "Watch and learn what befell your queen!"

The witch waved her hand and a whooshing sound came from the pool beneath her.

An instant later the pool went still. On its surface was the image of Queen Relna. She was dressed in silver robes and flying on a carpet over Sparr's black fortress.

Suddenly the sorcerer swooped in from nowhere, his cloak flapping like wings, the jagged fins behind his ears purple with rage.

"Queen of Droon!" Sparr yelled. "I have you now! Prepare to end your days!"

Relna swerved, but Sparr was too quick. He hurled a bolt of black fire at her.

Zzz — blam! Relna fell back and Sparr zoomed in, shrieking with mad laughter. "I have won!"

All of a sudden, the lake exploded.

Out of it burst the head of a giant serpent.

It was Demither!

"You will not harm her!" the witch boomed.

"Go back under the sea where you belong!" Sparr bellowed.

Blam! He shot a second fiery bolt at Queen Relna. She was thrown from her carpet and fell lifeless through the sky.

"Mother!" Keeah winced, watching the scene through her parted fingers.

But from Demither's eyes came a piercing red light. It surrounded the queen and slowed her fall. A moment later, the light vanished and something white fluttered up into the air.

A bird.

"The white falcon!" Keeah gasped. "That's how my mother became the falcon. You put a spell on her!"

In a final angry move, Sparr hurled a bolt of sizzling black fire at Demither. She took the blow in her heart and shrank back into the lake.

The scene blurred and vanished, and then the pool was just a pool again.

Keeah watched the water until there was nothing more to see. She stood there stunned, unable to speak. Finally, she turned to Demither.

"You saved my mother's life," she said softly. "You didn't have to, but you did. Why?"

Water splashed suddenly behind them.

"Demither saved me," said a voice, "because . . . she is my sister!"

Everyone turned. There, bobbing up from the depths of another pool was a sleek black dolphin.

They all knew who it was.

It was Queen Relna.

Six

The Puzzle's Pieces

Keeah ran to the pool, knelt, and hugged the dolphin. "Mother, Mother! Is it true?"

The queen nuzzled her daughter. "Yes, my love, it is true. Demither and I are sisters."

Keeah stared at her mother. "But how . . . why didn't you ever tell me?"

"I forbade her to tell you until you

needed to know," Demither said. "My story is a sad one."

Julie turned to Eric and Neal. "Talk about a day of surprises!"

Neal blinked. "So Witch Demither is now . . . *Aunt* Demither? That's fairly weird."

"Keeah, my love," said the dolphin queen, "long ago my sister and I shared the same powers, the same love of Droon. But she . . ."

Relna stopped, struggling to find the words.

"I chose the way of strength over that of family," Demither hissed from her throne. "Sparr offered me greater powers. I followed him. But I grew greedy. You see what has become of me. Now Sparr is coming here to reclaim the Red Eye once and for all —"

At that moment, a rumbling sound echoed into the dome. Everyone looked up to see a shadow spreading over the surface of the sea.

"The black ships," said Julie. "They're nearly here."

"It is Sparr's warriors, coming for the Eye," said Demither. "Alas, Om has made me weak. Now only Keeah has the power to seal the jewel in Doom Gate."

Keeah looked at her mother, then at the witch. "Me? What do you mean? Why me?"

Demither dived into the silver pool, then surfaced, her skin even paler than before.

"Wizardry alone cannot stop Sparr," she replied. "His magic is deeper, darker, *older* than Galen's. Seven years ago, Keeah, I told your mother this. She did not believe me. So I took you and fled through the tunnels that weave through Droon's underground —"

"The passages!" Eric gasped. "Of course! They connect every place to every other place. I fell into them once."

"It was in the passages that I gave you my powers," Demither said to the princess. "I knew you would need them to fight Sparr one day. But first you needed them for a dangerous journey."

"To the Upper World!" Neal blurted out. "Just like Eric remembered in his dream!"

"But why?" Keeah demanded of the witch. "*Why* did you take me to the Upper World? What was the dangerous journey? Tell me!"

Crash! Clang! Darkness swept over the dome.

The black ships were directly over the palace.

And the green water outside was turning red.

Red . . . with Ninns!

Hundreds of Lord Sparr's red-faced warriors were jumping into the water. They were riding fierce, dragon-tailed fish with spiky teeth and bulging yellow eyes. They dived swiftly to the palace.

"Ninns *plus* sea monsters!" cried Neal. "It just doesn't get any worse!"

Demither's eyes flashed. "They have come for the red jewel. Keeah, you alone, using all your powers together, can seal the Eye away from Sparr."

"But how will we get in the Doom Gate?" Keeah asked.

"You yourself are the key!" the witch said. "You will find the Gate in a grotto beneath this palace. In the Gate are three rooms. In the final chamber is a pit. You must seal the Eye in that pit. And remember — just as power can be shared, it can also be stolen. Be wary of Om. He is dangerous —"

Crash! The Ninns, with helmets looking like goldfish bowls on their heads, burst into the throne room. Water splashed wildly around them as they rushed in.

Keeah grasped the staff. Red light sizzled down the length of the staff to her hand.

She winced, but did not let go.

"Keeah, be strong," said her mother. Then she turned to Demither. "Sister, I will help you!"

"Get the Eye!" the Ninns grunted.

"No!" Relna declared. "Sparr will never get his hands on the jewel!"

"Take it, Keeah!" cried Demither. "Go now!"

As Ninn arrows whizzed into the throne room, the kids slipped away to the

narrow, twisting tunnels below the palace. Deeper and deeper they went, the light dimming around them, the sounds of fighting growing distant.

Finally the tunnels ended, opening into a large room carved from the jagged rock under the palace.

"This must be the grotto," said Keeah softly, trying to peer into the darkness.

With her friends close beside her, the princess grasped the staff tightly and stepped into the cave. When she did, a silvery glow lit up the darkness.

And they saw it.

"Whoa, it's big," said Neal with a low whistle.

Eric swallowed loudly.

"I think we found the Doom Gate."

Seven

The Gate Called Doom

The Doom Gate was a huge slab of stone. It stretched like a wall from the grotto floor to the high ceiling above.

A black door was set deep into the bottom of the Gate. In its center was a flat space in the shape of a hand.

"That must be the first of the three doors," said Eric. "We enter the Gate there."

"And you are the key," said Julie, remembering Demither's words.

"Then come on," the princess said. "Let's all stick together."

Eric smiled. "Like cheese on a pizza," he whispered to himself.

Keeah placed her hand flat against the center of the door.

Kkk! Boom — boom! The black door slid aside with a thunderous sound. Beyond it stood a smaller room carved from the rock around it.

But the instant they entered the room, the door clanged shut behind them.

"It's a trap!" said Julie, suddenly afraid. "I told you we shouldn't have gone in —"

Neal gave her a look. "No, you didn't."

Julie frowned. "Well, I was thinking it!"

"It's all right," said the princess, looking around. "Demither conjured the Doom

Gate to keep people out. I guess we should think of this as a sort of trial."

"A trial?" said Eric, glancing quickly at Julie and Neal. "I guess you could call it that."

He wondered if Keeah had any idea that she herself was being tested. She seemed brave and strong, but with so much magic in her, who could tell what would happen?

Especially in a place called Doom!

In the red light of the flickering Eye, they saw that the rocky room was very cold. Ice had formed all the way up the walls. A path winding to a second door across the room was matted with frost. Clusters of icicles hung from the ceiling.

"Well, we found Demither's freezer," said Neal, shivering. "But I don't think we'll find any ice cream."

Sssss! A hissing sound echoed off the walls.

"What was that?" Eric asked.

Keeah nodded. "I heard it, too."

Spar-r-r-r-r!

It was raspy and low. But whether it was more like an old man's voice, or like a whispering child's, Eric couldn't tell.

"Who said that?" said Julie, looking around.

The red jewel flared and sizzled in the staff.

Then they knew.

It was Om, the spirit in the stone.

Sparr made me. Demither stole me. You shall free me!

"Whoa, a jewel that talks," said Neal. "Well, think again, Eyeball. We're not freeing you. We're here to put you in your place!"

Are you him?

Neal blinked at the jewel. "Him who?"

No, it's not you. It's the other. The quiet one.

"Hey, is there an off switch on this thing?" Neal asked, backing onto the path. "Because he's starting to scare me —"

"Neal!" Julie cried. "Watch out!"

Suddenly — *crack! whoosh!* — a long, sharp icicle broke off from the ceiling and fell at Neal. Then another fell and another. He tried to jump away, but there was nowhere for him to go.

"Helllllllp!" he screamed.

Keeah thrust out her hands and — *zzzing!* Red light surrounded Neal. He flailed his arms and legs for an instant. Then — *ploomf!* — Neal was no longer Neal.

He was a turtle.

A baby sea turtle.

Crash! Crunch! Crack!

The icicles shattered on Neal's hard shell, sprinkling icy dust harmlessly across the floor.

Julie snatched Neal from the ground. "Keeah, you saved him! That was amazing!"

"Amazing?" Neal squeaked. "Amazing? It's terrible! Now I'm just like Queen Relna! I'll go from shape to shape. A chipmunk. An elephant. A worm! None of my clothes will fit —"

"Please don't freak out," said Eric.

"Neal, I'm sorry," said Keeah, touching his shell lightly. "I'm not sure where that spell came from. I know I can change you back, but not right now. We need to keep going."

Clang! Crash! The sounds of the battle in the palace echoed down into the cavern.

"And we need to go fast," said Eric.

"Wait here." Keeah held her hand up over her head and flicked her fingers. A shower of silver crystals fell over her, the flakes plinking and tinkling together like hundreds of tiny bells.

"What's that for?" Julie asked.

"Just watch," the princess said. She gazed up at the ceiling. "Here I go!"

There was a blur and a sudden whizzing sound where Keeah was. Then she was gone.

"Where did she go?" Neal started.

The next instant — *fwoosh!* — she was on the other side of the chamber, smiling brightly.

Then — *thwack! flang! crunch!* — every icicle fell from the ceiling and crashed to the floor right where Keeah had been just seconds earlier!

Eric blinked. "That was so cool!"

"It's safe for you to cross now," Keeah said.

Julie popped Neal into a small pouch on her belt, and she and Eric ran to the princess.

Keeah set her hand on the second door and it slid aside like the first.

But this time the room ahead was a warm green garden full of strange and beautiful plants.

"This looks much better," said Eric. "I think."

They stepped in carefully, Keeah in the lead.

"What's going on?" Neal asked in a squeaky voice, peering out of the pouch. "Anything happening?"

Just wait! hissed Om's voice.

Suddenly one of the plants nearest Eric unfurled two spiky tendrils and grabbed for him.

"Veggies!" cried Eric. "With attitude!"

He managed to dodge out of the way when the plant lunged. But Julie wasn't so lucky. The spiky shoots wrapped around her arms and yanked her off her feet.

"Ohhh!" she cried. The plant tightened its grip and twisted her upside down, sending Neal clattering to the floor.

Keeah jumped for the plant, muttering words in a language Eric had never heard before.

A red light covered Julie. She shuddered once, then — *poof!* — became a snake.

"A fire snake!" Keeah announced, surprised. "I didn't know I could do that, either."

Julie slithered easily from the plant's grasp. Then she turned and breathed on the plant.

Tssst! A blast of hot air withered the tendrils.

"Serves them right!" said Neal, snapping the toasted tendrils off with his beak. "Yum!"

Clang! Clonk! More sounds of fighting echoed into the Doom Gate.

"We'd better keep going," said Keeah. "Julie?"

"Spicy breath at your service!" Julie said. She slithered across the floor, burning a path of roasted plants to the far end of the room.

Eric wondered if Keeah's trial was going well. With two of his best friends turned into strange animals, he wasn't really sure.

He picked up Neal and popped him into the pouch on his belt. Then he tapped Keeah's arm.

"You can change Julie and Neal back, right?" he whispered. "Because I'm pretty sure their parents will be mad if I bring back a turtle and a snake instead of them."

"Of course!" Keeah said confidently. Then she whispered, "I hope so, anyway."

With that, she placed her hand on the final lock, the door slid aside with a *boom*, and they headed together into the last chamber.

Eight

The Spirit in the Stone

The innermost chamber of the Doom Gate was shrouded in shadows.

"Am I still in my shell?" asked Neal, poking his head out of Eric's pouch. "Or is this room dark?"

"It's-s-s dark," Julie hissed, coiling near Keeah's feet.

With a whispered word, the princess opened her palm, and a ball of blue wizard light rolled from her hand.

"Wizard powers are still the best," she said.

She tossed the ball high, lighting the chamber.

Right away, the light began to fade.

"There is magic in this place," Keeah said.

Eric peered into the gloom.

The chamber was almost perfectly round. A narrow stone bridge led from the door to a sort of island in the center. On either side of the bridge the ground fell away to nothing.

"I don't like it here," said Neal. "It makes me want to hide my head."

"Stay here, all of you," said Keeah. With the staff grasped firmly in her hand, she stepped onto the bridge. The others stayed near the door.

"This place makes me feel creepy," said Julie. "And for a s-s-snake, that's s-s-saying a lot!"

Eric felt it, too.

There was something frightening about this final chamber. He hoped Keeah wasn't as afraid as he and his friends were. It might mess up her powers just when she needed them most.

He watched Keeah closely.

As she crossed the bridge, a strange hot wind began swirling around the walls of the room.

It was coming from the staff. From Om.

"There's a pit in the center of the island," Keeah called. "And an iron lid that seals shut. That's where Om needs to go."

Eric hoped Keeah would be able to do it.

But Om didn't want to be inside the pit.

The closer Keeah drew to the pit, the fiercer were the sparks shooting off the end of the staff.

Flashes of red flame darted out of the

gem, circling the room and crackling over-head. The hot wind howled even louder.

Om was angry.

Eric stood by the door as Neal pulled his head into his shell and Julie curled up next to him.

"This is it," Eric murmured, watching Keeah. "This is her trial. And we can't help her. . . ."

On the island now, Keeah lifted the staff over her head. Then she turned the staff down toward the dark pit.

"Good-bye, Om," Keeah said. "The Red Eye goes dark . . . now!"

Noooo! Om howled. *Keeah! Look . . . look!*

The staff began to shake in her hands.

Eric tried to see what was happening, but the storm grew louder and darker and fiercer.

Keeah — look! Om whispered.

Suddenly there were castles forming out of the swirling wind, and piles of gold, and armies of warriors as far as the eye could see.

Use your witch power to set me free, Om shouted. *All this will be yours. Yes! Then I will share my power with you!*

"Or steal mine from me — like you stole Witch Demither's!" Keeah snapped.

You are part witch now!

"Begone, Om!" she cried. "Into the pit!"

Nooooo! Om shouted.

At once, the red storm swept around her.

"Keeah!" said Eric. He knew he wasn't supposed to help her. But he couldn't stop himself.

"Keeah!" he shouted. "Keeah!"

Eric battled the winds on the bridge. He

made his way across and leaped onto the island. Struggling to help Keeah, he, too, grasped the witch's staff.

You! Om shouted at him. *You!*

The staff felt strange in his hand. As if it were water running through his palm.

Hot water. Very hot!

Then he knew what it was. It was *power*.

"Owww!" cried Eric. "It's burning me!"

You are him, aren't you?

"What?" said Eric.

"I didn't say anything," said Keeah.

"Om did!" said Eric. "He's trying to scare me!"

Suddenly Om sent a blast of red light out from the Eye. The explosion struck Keeah and knocked her far from the pit.

She tumbled off the island.

"Keeah!" Eric cried.

Great howling noises filled the chamber. Wind tore at Eric. The island rumbled and shook.

"Keeah!" he called out. There was no answer.

A huge flame burst from the gem angrily and whirled around Eric as he clutched the staff.

You saw where they hid it.

"Keep quiet!" snapped Eric.

They, the princess and the witch. They hid it in your world. Seven years ago. You will find it.

"I don't think so!" Eric shouted angrily.

You will find it and bring it . . . to Sparr!

Eric's arms suddenly felt as heavy as stone. His head ached. He wanted to sleep. He felt weak all over. Just as Demither had felt weak.

He closed his eyes.

He felt his grip on the staff loosening.

Then he was falling . . . falling . . .

He dropped the staff . . . and fell off the island.

"Eric!" cried a familiar voice.

Suddenly Keeah was there.

Her long hair flying back, her face red from the heat of Om's anger, Keeah grabbed the staff.

Then she shot a beam of light at Eric.

He stopped falling.

The light flowed over him, flashing from her fingertips and into him. It was not the red light of witches that flowed over him.

It was the blue light of wizards.

The light surrounded Eric, and he felt suddenly strong. He flew up from the darkness as if by his own power.

He jumped back onto the island.

Together he and Keeah clutched the staff tight and, with one mighty thrust, they threw it deep into the pit.

Noooo! Om howled.

Red fire leaped out of the pit. But a bright blue burst of light forced it back.

Then, with a loud and final *wump!* Keeah kicked the thick black lid over the pit.

Instantly, the storm vanished. Om went silent. The Red Eye went dark. The chamber was still.

Eric looked over at the princess. His knees felt as if they were made of jelly.

She stared down at the pit and tried to catch her breath. Finally she spoke. "Well, that was something."

Eric laughed. It was strange to hear himself laugh, but that was all he could do. "That was something, all right! You did it!"

"No," she said. "We did it. Together. I just hope I didn't hurt you with that blast of light."

Eric shook his head. "Actually, it felt great!"

Together they walked back over the

bridge to Neal and Julie, who lay fast asleep near the door.

Keeah closed her eyes, her face going still. "Okay, then," she said. Murmuring some strange words, she held her hands over them.

A moment later — *poof!* — Neal and Julie were not only awake, they were themselves again.

"Did anything happen?" asked Neal, stretching his neck.

Eric shot a smile at Keeah. "Not too much."

"Then we'd better get back to the dome," said Julie, doing a little wiggle. "My snake hearing was telling me that the fighting is worse."

As they headed back through the door, Eric turned one last time. The dark lid over the pit glowed for an instant, as if it were red-hot.

And he thought he heard Om whisper once more before the chamber went black.

"Eric, come on," said Keeah. "Our battle isn't over yet."

Eric turned from the chamber and trotted over to her. As he did, a smile broke out on his face. Keeah had won at least one battle right there. The wizard in her had won out over the witch.

Keeah had passed her trial.

"Come on," he said. "Let's boot those Ninns back where they came from. No jewel for them. They're going home empty-handed!"

"Yahoo!" Neal yelled. "Now you're talking!"

"Let's go!" cried Julie.

Nine

Ninns in the Grotto

Cheering loudly, the four friends raced back through the three doors of the Doom Gate.

They charged out into the big grotto.

And stopped dead.

"Uh-oh," muttered Neal. "Talk about battles not over yet . . ."

Om's rumbling and storming had cracked the walls of the grotto. Water was rushing in from outside. A whole ocean of water.

So were Ninns, hundreds of them, riding in on their sharp-toothed fish monsters. The spiky tails on each fish whipped about wildly as the waves washed them in.

"Helmets on," said Eric. "We're going underwater!"

There was a dull *thunk* as the first Ninn arrow struck the Doom Gate behind their heads.

"Don't those Ninns have anything better to do than attack us?" Julie asked.

"Attack them!" bellowed the chief Ninn.

"Guess not!" said Keeah. "I'll just have to stop them the old-fashioned way. With a spell."

She raised her hands and flicked her fingers at the charging Ninns.

Fzzz. A tiny spray of blue sparks left her fingers, traveled a few inches in the air, sputtered, then faded.

Neal was nodding slowly as he watched the Ninns advance. "Okay. Now really do it."

Keeah's eyes grew big. "I can't. My battle with Om must have weakened me."

Neal was still nodding. "Then could I be a turtle again? *Because I need somewhere to hide!*"

The Ninns surrounded them on every side and began pushing them back against the Gate.

"Now what do we do?" asked Eric.

"I know what I'm going to do," said Neal. "I'm going to freak out. I've been holding off because the timing wasn't right. But now I'm going to freak out and I don't care who sees it!"

Eric saw Neal's finger go for his belt. "Neal — don't! Remember what Friddle said —"

Neal pressed the red button on his sea belt.

Whoomf! A tiny jet of flame burst suddenly from the back of Neal's sea belt.

"Whoa — it's hot!" he cried. Before he had a chance to say anything else, he blasted straight through the front line of Ninns.

Flimp! Bloink! Ooof! Yeowwww!

Screaming, Neal whizzed around the grotto at lightning speed, leaving a trail of foamy water and toppled Ninns behind him.

"Help!" he cried as he zipped by his friends. "Can't control it — *glub!* — need — help!"

He blasted through another bunch of Ninns and zoomed up the tunnel to the throne room.

"Well, he freaked out," said Julie. "But he escaped."

"We need to get out of here, too," said Keeah.

"Too late for that!" growled a deep voice.

A rush of bubbles burst in their faces, and three fat Ninns charged in on their fierce sea beasts.

"Get the princess!" the Ninns grunted.

"Never!" said a familiar voice.

Suddenly — *thwump!* — the Ninns and their creatures went crashing into the grotto wall as a smooth black shape swam out of nowhere.

It was a dolphin!

"Mother!" Keeah exclaimed, rushing to her.

The Ninns shouted and grumbled inside their fishbowl helmets. But they sped off quickly.

"Follow me," the dolphin queen said. "Demither needs us, all of us."

With a wiggle of her flippers, Relna motioned for Keeah to climb onto her long, sleek back. "Let's go!"

Speeding ahead, Relna bumped Ninns out of the way, clearing a path for Eric and Julie.

Eric looked at his friend. "Well, should we freak out, too?"

Julie grinned. "It's the only way!"

They both hit the red buttons on their belts.

Whoomf-whoomf!

They shot across the grotto after Keeah and her mother. Together they rocketed up through the water-filled tunnels and finally back into Demither's throne room, where they met up with Neal.

Ker-splash! Eric and Julie broke through

the water's surface and shot straight up to the dome.

"How — do — we — stop?" Julie cried.

"Try — pressing — the — button — again!" shouted Neal, who was still zooming around.

They all pressed the red button a second time.

The three friends smashed against the inside of the dome — *splat!* — their jets died — *fzzzzt!* — they plummeted straight to the ground and dropped right into Demither's pool — *splash!*

When they jumped to their feet they saw that Demither's guards had pushed the Ninns from the throne room.

But that wasn't the biggest news.

The biggest news was Demither.

She was turning into a sea monster.

Ten

The Wizard Queen

Demither's tail, now long and spiky, splashed wildly in the pool beneath the throne.

Her eyes, sunken before, were now gleaming red. Her skin was turning crusty and covered with spikes.

Claws were growing where fingers had been.

"Sparr is casting his spell over me once

more," the witch said. "He is near — so near!"

"We will help you," said Relna.

"There is no time," Demither replied. "Keeah, come to me quickly. Together we will release the queen from her spell."

Keeah looked at her mother.

"You must trust her," said Relna.

Wump! Wump! The Ninns were using pieces of the wrecked ship to batter on the dome.

Keeah took Demither's hand.

Kkkkk! Blue light from the princess mixed with the red light of the witch and became a shimmering purple. Then the light flowed outward to the dolphin, swirling around it.

As the light encircled the queen, Relna's black skin turned ashen, then as bright as sunlight. Then the dolphin vanished.

"But where — " Keeah said.

A moment later — *slooosh!* — there was a sudden spray of crystal water. A fountain of light and air and wind filled the dome.

When it cleared, Relna stood before them, a queen once more.

"She's beautiful!" gasped Julie.

Relna was dressed in a long wizard's cloak. It was all pearly white and stitched with glittering quarter-moons of gold and blue.

Around her head sat a crown of diamonds.

Even though her eyes told of many years of trial and heartache, she beamed at her daughter.

"Mother!" said Keeah, running into her arms. "I've waited so long for you!"

"One curse ended," Demither said

softly, "another begins. Sparr will take me now —"

Ka-foom! The Ninns blasted into the dome once more. Demither's guards rushed to them.

But the Ninns kept coming. Hundreds of them. They charged in, filling the palace.

Keeah turned to the witch. "You said you gave me your powers for a dangerous journey. Tell me now — why did we go to the Upper World?"

The witch's face had changed again. It was now as terrifying as Relna's was beautiful. "You will learn when the time is right, not before!"

Eric looked at Demither's cold expression. He remembered what Om had told him.

Keeah had no memory of it. But together she and Demither had hidden something in the Upper World.

And Om said Eric would find it.

With a final push, hundreds of heavy-footed red warriors blew past Demither's guards and surrounded the witch.

"Sparr wants you now!" the warriors grunted. They quickly threw an iron net over her and pulled her away.

"Beware the sorcerer!" Demither shouted. "He could be anyone! Beware . . . beware!"

Splash!

A dark wave swept into the throne room. On the wave rode the snakey creature with the stubby red snout. It slithered into the throne room, hissing and growling.

"Galen?" said Julie.

"Eerrgh!" the creature growled. Its burning eyes flashed at the children, then it turned and vanished into the dark sea again.

The witch struggled briefly in her net, then was dragged into the darkness by the Ninns.

"I will find you!" Relna called to her sister. "I will never give up hope!"

A moment later, the witch was gone, the Ninns were gone, and the undersea world was quiet, peaceful, and still.

Even Demither's guards had disappeared into the far corners of the green city.

"It is over," said Queen Relna. "We must go."

Linking their hands, Keeah and her mother whispered strange words together. Surrounded by a glistening bubble of air, Queen Relna, Keeah, and the three friends then left the dome and floated away from the witch's realm.

Breaking the surface, they found Friddle's plane — its wings folded up on the sides — rocking gently on the waves.

Darkness was now passing away from the water and the land. The hurricane had vanished.

It seemed like a new day.

"Welcome, Queen Relna, to my humble craft!" the inventor said, helping them aboard, then giving the queen a deep bow. "I was as worried as anything! Besides, the yip-yips were getting quite restless —"

All of a sudden the two blue fur balls jumped out of their cage and — *ploof-ploof!* — instead of yip-yips, two figures appeared before them.

"Galen!" exclaimed Keeah. "And Max!"

"We could not stay away," said the wizard.

"And the only way I could stop him from meddling," chirped Max, "was to go with him!"

"My queen!" said the wizard, bowing his white head. "We are all at your service."

Relna smiled at her old friend. "I see Droon has been in good hands."

"Keeah has indeed done well today," Galen said. "And against such terrible odds!" Then he hugged the princess and her mother tightly.

As he did, Julie stared at him, then at the dark water below, then at Galen again.

"Wait a second . . . if you were up here the whole time, then who was that ugly monster down there —" Julie stopped. She jumped.

"Oh! It was him, wasn't it? It was Sparr! He's even uglier now. And I thought he was you! Oh! I bopped him! I bopped Sparr! With this hand!"

"Julie, don't freak out," said Neal with a grin.

"You'd better wash that hand," said Eric.

Julie plunged it into the water. "Eeew! Yuck!"

Laughing, Keeah turned to her mother. Her smile faded. "Sparr will come back, won't he?"

The queen looked out across the sea. The last of the Ninn ships was disappearing over the horizon. "Yes," she said, "but in what form, we do not know."

"Keeah, you have learned much today," Galen added. "You were tempted by the dark forces but did not bend to them. You have acted far older than your years."

Keeah beamed at first, then frowned. "But does having powers mean I have to grow up? That I can't have fun anymore?"

"Ha!" said the old wizard, smiling under his snow-white beard. "I think you are getting a tiny bit ahead of yourself, Princess. There is still much for you to learn. For instance, Quill wrote something after you left. The legendary Hob has gotten loose again. And we must all go in search of him."

Keeah blinked. "Hob? I never heard of Hob."

Galen grinned. "Of course not — he is one of the best-kept secrets of Droon!"

Neal turned to Eric. "Why do I get the feeling that there are tons of secrets about Droon?"

"And that it will take about a million years to learn them all?" added Julie.

Keeah put her arms around her friends. "I guess this means I'll be seeing you soon."

Eric laughed. "Real soon!"

Max pointed to the nearby coast. The magical staircase was resting on the very top of the cliffs. "Your world calls you back again," he chirped. "At least for a little while."

Friddle giggled. "Which means that I need my yips-yips back! Max? Galen?"

Ploof-ploof! The wizard and his spider troll helper were suddenly blue fur balls again. They hopped into their cage and began to run.

As they did, the plane lifted up over the waves and flew toward the cliffs of Mintar.

The orange sun of afternoon peeked out behind the last few clouds. It shone across the green water and made even Demither's scary realm seem peaceful.

Friddle landed next to the shimmering stairs.

"Farewell, friends of Droon!" said Queen Relna, giving each of the kids a special hug.

"I hope you have sweet dreams," added Keeah. She smiled as they started up the stairs.

Neal ran up the steps first, waving to Keeah and Friddle and Queen Relna.

" 'Bye, yip-yips!" Julie called out.

"Yip! Yip!" said Galen and Max.

"Hey, guys," said Neal, when his friends joined him halfway up the stairs. "How about a nice, normal day of just hanging out? No magic. Just us. What do you say?"

Julie smiled. "A nice, normal day? That sounds soooo good!"

Eric laughed, feeling lighter than air as he chased his friends to the top of the stairs. Then, turning, he raised his hands to wave at Keeah one more time.

That was when he saw the faint blue sparks shooting from the tips of his fingers.

ABOUT THE AUTHOR

Tony Abbott is the author of more than two dozen funny novels for young readers, including the popular *Danger Guys* books and the *Weird Zone* series. Since childhood he has been drawn to stories that challenge the imagination, and, like Eric, Julie, and Neal, he often dreamed of finding doors that open to other worlds. Now that he is older — though not quite as old as Galen Longbeard — he believes he may have found some of those doors. They are called books. Tony Abbott was born in Ohio and now lives with his wife and two daughters in Connecticut.

For more information about Tony Abbott and the continuing saga of Droon, please visit tonyabbottbooks.com.